MICHAEL MORPURGO

Illustrated by Trevor Stubley

Friend or Foe

David and Tucky hated being evacuated
from their London home during the wartime
bombing. Now the other children at their
new country school make fun of them and
call them townies.

But Mr and Mrs Reynolds soon have them
caught up in their new life on the farm, and
it's David and Tucky, not the other
children, who see the German plane crash.

Also by Michael Morpurgo

for younger readers

Friend or Foe
Michael Morpurgo

mammoth

First published by Macmillan Education Ltd 1977
Magnet edition published 1984
Reprinted 1985, 1986 and 1988
First published 1989 by Mammoth
Reissued 1990 by Mammoth
an imprint of Egmont Children's Books Limited
239 Kensington High Street, London W8 6SA

Reprinted 1991
Reissued 1992
Reprinted 1993 (three times), 1994 (three times), 1995 (twice),
1996 (twice), 1997 (four times), 1998 (three times), 1999

Text copyright © 1977 Michael Morpurgo

ISBN 0 7497 0130 7

A CIP catalogue record for this title
is available from the British Library

Printed and bound in Great Britain
by Cox & Wyman Ltd, Reading, Berkshire

For Bess and Julie

Friend or Foe

1

His mother woke him as usual that morning, shaking his shoulder and then kissing him gently as he rolled over. It was pitch black around him, but then he was used to that by now. For months they had slept down in the cellar on the bunks his father had made the last time he was home on leave.

'Here's your apple, dear,' his mother said. 'Sit up and have your apple now.' And she patted the pillow behind him as he pushed himself up on to his elbows. He felt the saucer come into his hand. His early morning apple was the only thing that had not changed since the war started. Every morning as far back as he could remember his mother had woken him this way – with an apple peeled, cored and quartered lying opened up on a white saucer.

He felt his mother shifting off the bed and watched for the flare of yellow light as she struck the match for the oil lamp. The cellar walls flickered and then settled in the new light, and the boy saw his mother was dressed to go out. She had her coat on and her hat with the brown feather at the back. It was only then that he remembered. His stomach turned over inside him and tears choked at his throat. The morning he had thought would never come, had come. Every night since he'd first heard about it, he prayed it might not happen to him; and the night before, he had prayed he would die in his sleep rather than wake up and have to go.

'You were restless again last night, dear. Did you sleep?' He nodded, not trusting himself to speak. 'Come on now. Eat your apple and get dressed. Quick as you can, dear. It's six o'clock by the station, they said. It's a quarter-to now. I left you as long as I could.'

Fifteen minutes left. Fifteen minutes and he'd be gone. Thirty minutes and she would be back in this house without him. She was bending over him, shaking his shoulder. 'Please, dear. We must hurry. Eat it down, quickly now. Miss Roberts said you'd be having a roll and jam on the train, but you must have something before you go.'

'Don't want it, Mum.' He handed the saucer back to her. Only moments before he had been savouring that first bite of his apple. They were always crisp, always juicy, like

2

nothing else. But now he felt sick at the sight of it.

'You must, David. You always have your apple. You know you do.'

He had upset her and ate it to make her happy, swallowing it like medicine, trying not to taste it. Each bite reminded him that this was the last apple.

Once out of bed he dressed to keep the cold out. His mother was packing his suitcase and he watched everything going in and wondered where he'd be when he took it all out again.

'They said only one case, so there's only room for one change of clothes. All the things you wanted, they're at the bottom. I'll send on the rest as soon as I know where you'll be.' She smoothed down his coat collar and brushed through his hair with her fingers. 'You'll do,' she said, smiling softly.

'Do I have to, Mum? Do I have to go?' Even as he asked he knew it was useless. Everyone was going from school – no one was staying behind. He was ashamed of himself now. He'd promised himself he'd be brave when he said goodbye. He clung to his mother, pressing his face into her coat, fighting his tears.

She crouched down in front of him, holding him by the shoulders. 'You remember what I said, David, when I told you your father had been killed? Do you?' David nodded. 'I said you'd have to be the man in the house, remember?' He took the handkerchief she was offering. 'You never saw your father crying, did you?'

'No, Mum.'

'Men don't cry, see? Try to be a man, David, like your father was, eh?' She chucked him under the chin, and straightened the cap on to the front of his head. 'Come on now. We'll be late.'

It was still dark up in the street, and a fine drizzle sprayed their faces as they walked away from the house. David looked back over his shoulder as they came to the postbox at the corner and caught a last glimpse of the front steps. He felt his mother's hand on his elbow, and then they were round the corner.

Ahead of them there was a glow of fire in the sky. 'South of the river,' his mother said. 'Battersea, I should say. Poor devils. At least you'll be away from all that, David, away from the bombs, away from the war. At least they won't get you as well.' He was surprised by the grim tone in her voice.

'Where will you go, Mum?'

'Wherever they send me. Probably to the coast – Kent or somewhere like that. Somewhere where there's anti-aircraft guns, that's all I know. Don't worry, I'll write.'

Their footsteps sounded hollow in the

empty street. They had to step off the pavement to pick their way round the edge of a pile of rubble that was still scattered halfway across the street. That was where the Perkins family had lived. They had been bombed out only a week before; they were all killed. Special prayers were said at school assembly for Brian and Garry Perkins, but no one ever mentioned them after that. They were dead, after all.

In the gloom outside Highbury and Islington Underground Station there was already a crowd of people. Miss Evers' voice rang out above the hubbub and the crying. She was calling out names. His mother pulled at his hand and they ran the last few yards.

'Tony Tucker. Tony Tucker.' Miss Evers' voice rose to a shriek. 'Where's Tucky? Has anyone seen Tucky?'

'He's coming, miss. I saw him.'

'And what about David Carey? Is he here yet?'

'Yes, miss. I'm here, miss.' David spoke out, pleased at the strength in his voice.

'Here's Tucky, miss. He's just coming.'

'Right then.' Miss Evers folded her piece of paper. 'We're all here, and it's time to go. Say goodbye as quick as ever you can. The train leaves Paddington at half past eight, and we have to be there at least an hour before. So hurry it up now – and don't forget your gas masks.'

David felt the case being handed to him. 'Goodbye, David. And don't worry. It'll be all right. I'll send a letter as soon as I can. God bless.' She kissed him quickly on the cheek and turned away. He watched her until she disappeared at the end of the street. All around him there was crying: boys he'd never dreamt could cry, weeping openly, and mothers holding on to each other as they walked away. He was glad his mother hadn't cried, and it helped him to see so many of his friends as miserable as he felt himself. He blinked back the tears that had gathered in his eyes and wiped his face before turning towards the station.

The warmth of the Underground came up to meet them as the school trooped down the silent, unmoving escalator. They followed Miss Evers along the tunnels, down the stairways and out on to the platform. Tucky came up alongside David and dropped his suitcase.

'H'lo, Davey.'

'H'lo, Tucky.' They were old friends and there was nothing more to be said.

They did not have long to wait. There was a distant rumble and then a rush of warm, oily wind that blew their eyes closed as it rushed into the platform. Miss Evers counted

them as they pushed and jostled into the carriage, herding them in like sheep, so that every corner of the carriage was filled. The doors clicked and hissed shut, and the train jerked forward, throwing everyone against each other.

David watched the last Highbury and Islington sign as long as he could, craning his neck until the carriage plunged into the darkness of the tunnel and it was gone.

'That's that, then,' said Tucky next to him. David nodded and looked up at the parallel rows of handles that swung from the roof of the carriage, always out of reach. And he remembered his father lifting him up high above everyone, and how he'd hung on to the strap next to his father's looking down on a sea of upturned faces.

Miss Evers was shouting at them again. 'Boys, boys. Can you all hear me, boys? Sam, you're not listening. I can see you're not listening. You can't listen and talk at the same time – it's not possible. Now, we've been through all this many times before, but I'll do it just once more to make sure. We're going to . . . where are we going, Tucky?'

'Devon, miss.'

'What station do we have to go to, to get to Devon, Tucky?'

'Don't know, miss.'

'Paddington, Tucky. We're going to Paddington Station.' Whenever Miss Evers wanted to tell them all something, she always asked Tucky first; and when Tucky didn't know, and he never did know, that was her excuse to tell them herself. She picked on Tucky mercilessly, and David hated her for it.

'And what am I going to give you at Paddington Station, Tucky? Can you remember that, Tucky?'

'No, miss.'

'Your placards, Tucky. With your name and address on. Remember? In case you get lost.'

'And the string, miss,' someone else said. Tucky was already sniffing, his hands screwed into his eyes. Another question from Miss Evers and he would dissolve into floods of tears.

'Well, I'm glad someone was paying attention. Placards and string. You'll be wearing the placards round your neck. Remember now, Tucky?' Tucky nodded into his raincoat sleeve, and Miss Evers left him alone after that.

They had to change trains once and Sam left his case behind on the train. Miss Evers screamed at the guard and the doors hissed open again and she went back in for it. When she came out she screamed at Sam, but Sam braved it out and then grinned sheepishly as soon as her back was turned.

Placards strung round their necks, and two

by two, the boys climbed the long stairs up into Paddington Station. David and Tucky were almost last in the crocodile and as far away from Miss Evers as possible.

Up to that moment it had been just his school that was being evacuated, but now David discovered that every other child in London seemed to be at the station. Miss Evers shouted back at them to hold on to the belt of the boy in front and they wound their way like a long snake through the crowds of milling children and screaming teachers, who paused only to blow their whistles. And above it all came the thunder and rhythmic pounding of steam engines, and the rich, exciting smell of the smoke.

David had been on a train once before. Just before the war started he'd been on a school journey to Birchington, but then his mother and father had been on the platform waving him off. He felt the belt in his hand jerk and the crocodile stuttered forward again towards the platform.

Miss Roberts, the headmistress, was waiting for them by the ticket barrier; and so was Miss Hardy. Miss Roberts was in her usual bird's nest hat, and Miss Hardy, as usual, was clucking around her like a worried hen. Miss Evers seemed relieved to see them, and smiled for the first time that morning. Miss

Roberts took charge and beckoned everyone closer.

'The train's at least two hours late, boys, so we'll have to wait. Put your cases down and sit on them.' It was good to have Miss Roberts there in her hat and bright clothes. There wasn't a boy in the school who didn't like her, and now her smiles and laughter were familiar and comforting in the strangeness and noise of the station.

David spent the two hours chatting to Tucky and looking at everyone else – that was all there was to do. The marches blared out of the loudspeakers, but they were so loud he could hardly make out the tune – and when there was a tune he recognised, a great explosion of steam would ruin it for him. Miss Hardy gave everyone a roll and jam with a mug of warm milk, and Miss Roberts sat heavily on her suitcase and smoked her way through a packet of cigarettes.

It seemed as if the train would never leave, but it did – three hours late. The boys piled into the train, fourteen to a carriage, and the train stood there, hissing gently.

David and Tucky found themselves sitting in Miss Roberts' carriage. They knew it would mean cigarette smoke all the way to Devon, but that was better than Miss Hardy's fussing, and a lot better than Miss Evers' waspish tongue. Miss Roberts collected all their plac-

12

ards and put them in the luggage rack above their heads.

'You won't need those for a bit. I think I know who you all are.' Miss Roberts sat down next to Tucky, and the seat sank. 'You'll need them again when we get to Devon – if we ever do.' She took off her bird's nest hat with a flourish and shook out her red hair, and then settled down to a packet of Senior Service cigarettes and a pile of orange paperbacks.

She was a huge lady, and Tucky wondered if he would ever be able to stop himself from sliding down towards her into the crater she had made in the cushioned seat.

Doors were banging all the way down the train and a group of sailors ran past waving and shouting. More banging, the shrill whistle, the pressure building up in short blasts of steam; and then the train heaved forward, the engine settling into a slow pulling rhythm as they watched the platform slip away.

'We're off,' said Tucky.

'On our way, boys,' said Miss Roberts. 'Say goodbye to London, and good luck. Not for ever, you know. We'll be back.'

David stared out of the window and wondered what his mother was doing at that moment and how long it would be before he'd see her again.

2

It rained all the way from London to Exeter. Miss Roberts hardly lifted her head from her books, unless it was to pull out another packet of cigarettes from her handbag. David and Tucky played noughts and crosses until they ran out of paper, and they were left staring at the window waiting for the next stop.

David passed the time by tracing drops of rain as they ran in intricate and erratic patterns from the top of the windowpane down towards the bottom. He would find two or three droplets that began life at the same time at the top, and watch them race each other to the bottom; and sometimes they would join together and plummet down in a great flood.

They stopped frequently and that did help to break the monotony of the journey; and lunch of a sandwich and a biscuit at Westbury was a chance to stretch their legs and to empty the carriage of Miss Roberts' cigarette smoke.

But lunch was Tucky's downfall. He began to go white almost as soon as the train pulled out of Westbury, and a few minutes later was as sick as a dog. Miss Roberts did her best, but there were no corridors on the train, so all she could do was to hold his head, while the rest of them tried to keep as far away as possible. It was all cleared up at the next stop, but the after-smell still hung on, and Tucky's face was still a pale shade of green. He looked dreadful, and David tried to ignore him and to concentrate on the line of the hills in the distance. He thought it looked like the pictures of Devon he'd been shown at school, but they were still hours away from Exeter, and as the journey dragged on, his thoughts returned again to his house in Islington.

Tucky was feeling better. 'My mum said it won't be long,' he said suddenly. David said nothing. 'She said the war would be over in a few months and we'd all be home again. So it won't be long, will it?'

'Depends on who wins it.' David said.

'We'll win it,' Paul Browning said from the other side of the carriage. 'Everyone says we'll win it.'

'Then it'll be a long war.'

'Who says?' Paul was sneering.

'That's what my dad said,' David replied quietly. He hated mentioning his father, and he hadn't meant to. He felt vulnerable now.

15

'He said that if the Germans win it'll be a short war and if we win it'll be long.'

'But we won last time,' Tucky piped up. 'We won then, didn't we?'

'Yeah. He's right,' Paul was leaning forward. 'We won all right, and what you can do once, you can do again. That's right, isn't it, miss?'

'What is, Paul?' Miss Roberts looked up.

'The war, miss. Davey says we won't win it. You heard him, miss. We beat them last time, so we will again. Stands to reason, doesn't it miss?'

Miss Roberts closed her book. 'No, Paul. It doesn't stand to reason.' She sounded firm, and everyone listened when she sounded firm. 'I think we shall win in the end, I certainly hope we do. But it will not be in a few weeks or a few months. It may take a long long time to win – a year, two or three years, who knows? You must understand that you will not be going home for some time. You'll have a new home and a new school and it won't be easy for you. But it will be a lot easier if you can understand that you won't be going home for a long time. One day we'll all go back to Islington, but not for a long time. Understand?'

It could not have been clearer. David had won his duel with Paul, but it gave him no pleasure. He would gladly have lost one little argument for some ray of hope from Miss Roberts. There was none. The carriage fell silent and remained that way until the train pulled into Exeter Station. It was dark already and they were hungry.

Placards were put on, cases checked, and then they were on the platform, and out into the cold. Tucky and David stuck together while Miss Roberts gathered the whole school around her for a roll call. Then she led the way through the ticket barrier and towards a waiting bus. There were people everywhere, but it was not like the bustle and noise at Paddington. Here they were standing and staring solemnly as the boys straggled through the ticket hall.

'Where you boys from, my dear?' The ticket collector put his hand on David's shoulder and turned him round.

'London,' said David.

'I know that, my dear,' he laughed easily. 'I know that right enough. But whereabouts in London?'

David felt foolish, and flushed. 'Islington,' said Tucky.

'Not heard of that, have you?' He asked around him and everyone shook their head. 'Off you go then, my dear, and keep smiling.' David did not know what he should be smiling about, and he could not help wondering how anyone could have reached the age of

that ancient ticket collector without ever
having heard of Islington.

'Talk funny, don't they?' said Tucky, as
they rushed after the others.

Miss Roberts marshalled them into the dark
green coach in the station yard, and David sat
with Tucky on the long bench seat at the back

19

and waited. They all waited, but nothing happened. Then someone realised the driver was missing, and a policeman went off in the dark to look for him. The boys sat numbed in their seats, every one of them exhausted, too exhausted even to be homesick. The driver came back eventually, and there were angry words in front of the bus – Miss Evers was giving him a piece of her mind.

The blackout was in force, and the headlights of the bus were hooded so that only a thin slit of light struck the road ahead. The engines throbbed underneath them and the bus moved at last.

The journey through the dark lanes seemed unending. David sensed they must be out in the countryside because there were no houses. All he could see were high hedges and the occasional glimpse of a field as the headlights skimmed over it through a gateway. No one spoke in the bus. It was too noisy, but no one felt like it anyway. Tucky had gone to sleep on David's shoulder, but kept waking up every few minutes to ask if they were there. Halfway down the coach David could make out the shape of Miss Roberts' hat as it was lit up from time to time by the glow of her cigarette.

'This is it,' the driver's voice shouted, and the coach slowed down. Tucky woke up with a start. 'Round this bend and you're here.'

'Placards and cases,' said Miss Roberts. 'Don't leave anything behind.'

'And don't forget your cases, children,' Miss Hardy echoed. 'Make sure it's your own case and no one else's. Check them now, children.'

The bus had stopped, but David could see nothing out of the windows. He rubbed an island clear of steam and peered through. They were in a small square surrounded by low buildings. A door was thrown open in the darkness and a shaft of yellow light flooded out towards the coach.

'Everyone out.' Miss Roberts walked sideways down the centre of the coach. 'And mind your manners now.'

The lights of the village hall were blinding at first and David blinked and squinted his way down the hall. There were faces all around him, peering red faces and eyes that followed him. He looked away and followed on up some wooden steps and on to a platform. There were two long benches and David found himself in the back row and Tucky slid in next to him. It was warm in the hall and from somewhere came the smell of tomato soup, red tomato soup.

It was thick and not too hot, and they were each given a great chunk of brown bread which they dunked into the white enamel cups. David ate his slowly, savouring the warmth. Every new mouthful sent comforting shivers down his body. He had hoped for some of Tucky's but clearly Tucky was feeling well enough now to finish his. Then there were cheese rolls, and they washed it all down with the sweetest cocoa David had ever tasted. The cocoa was too much for Tucky and he emptied his into David's mug, and David crouched over it warming his hands.

Down in the hall everyone had stopped talking and Miss Roberts was speaking. 'The boys have all had a very long day, and I think we should get them off to bed as quickly as we can. But I know they'd all like me to thank you kind people for our welcoming meal. It's a long time since we've eaten like that. Now most of you are having one boy to stay and some two or three. Do choose quickly. They're a good bunch of boys, and I know you'll look after them as well as you can. You'll find their names and ages on their placards, so as soon as you've chosen the one you're having, please register with Miss Evers at the table by the door. That way we'll know where everyone has gone to. It wouldn't do to lose anyone now, would it? Take the first row first and then the back row will move forward.'

The crowd of faces in the hall moved in closer, looking up at them. The children sat sipping their cocoa and gazed back down at them. There was a lot of whispering and it was a long time before anyone moved. Then one of the ladies stepped forward and peered closely for a moment at Paul's placard. She smiled up at him over her glasses.

'Come on then, Paul,' she said, tapping him on the knee. 'Let's get the ball rolling. You come along with me.'

'Yes, miss,' said Paul and looked to Miss Roberts for reassurance. Miss Roberts nodded.

'Off you go then, Paul. And be good now.' Miss Roberts spoke kindly, and Paul got up and walked down the steps into the hall. The lady took his case and the two of them walked away towards Miss Evers' table at the back of the hall.

'Doesn't know what she's in for,' Tucky whispered from behind his cocoa mug. And David smiled for the first time that day. He sipped his cocoa and looked around the hall, trying to pick out a face he liked, but there were too many people and they were too remote to be real.

It was a smooth enough business after that. One by one the chairs on the platform emptied and soon the whole front row was gone. Miss Roberts beckoned the back row into their places.

Sam went. Billy Preston and Graham Watts went together, and gradually the hall was emptying. There was a small knot by the registration table, and Miss Roberts was with them. There was something wrong, David could tell that. Everyone kept glancing back up at the platform where David and Tucky sat side by side at the end of the front row. There was no one left.

'I'm sorry, Miss Roberts,' one of the ladies was saying. 'I'm sorry, but there's been an upset.'

'They have to sleep somewhere, don't they?' Miss Roberts sounded crisp. They were speaking in that urgent half-whisper that adults use when they don't want to alarm listening children.

"Tis Mr Reynolds out to Hamleigh Farm. He's not come in to collect. They were all told. Half past eight he was told, like the rest. 'Tis past eleven now. Can't think where he's to.'

'But even with Mr Reynolds, that still leaves one boy unaccounted for,' Miss Roberts insisted.

'That'll be all right, you'll see, my dear. We'll find him somewhere. Poor little scrap.'

Tucky leaned closer to David. 'Davey. If they can't find anyone to look after us, will they send us home, d'you think?'

'Doubt it.'

'But what will they do with us then?'

'Miss Roberts will see us right,' David said hopefully. 'Don't worry, she'll see to it.'

'Davey. Why do you think no one chose us?' Tucky droned on in his flat voice.

'They didn't choose me, 'cos you were sitting next to me, and they didn't choose you because I was sitting next to you. And besides, we're not the prettiest in the class, are we?' He tried to joke it away, but he was hurt inside just as Tucky was. Time and time again people had looked him over and passed him by. 'Anyway,' he went on, 'I didn't much like the look of them.'

'Nor me,' said Tucky. 'Nor me.'

The arguing at the other end of the hall had dwindled to an inaudible whisper now as they all realised the two boys might overhear them. But the longer it went on, the more obvious it became that the situation was serious. No one else seemed to have room for an evacuee, and it looked very much as if Mr Reynolds might not be coming at all. Finally Miss Roberts suggested they should give the boys a bed in the hall for the night, and someone went off to look for mattresses and blankets. Miss Hardy looked as if she would burst into tears at any minute, and Miss Evers kept throwing up her hands in disgust. Meanwhile David and Tucky sat alone up on the platform, too tired and bewildered even to care what happened to them.

They had pulled away the chairs to make room for the newly arrived mattresses and bedding when the hall door banged open. A huge, bearded man in a great woolly coat and knee-high gaiters strode into the hall followed by a rangy-looking black and white sheepdog. Everyone gawped.

'I'm sorry to be late, but I've come for a boy.'

'You are Mr Reynolds I presume.' Miss Evers' voice was stiff with anger.

'I am, my dear, and who may you be?'

'Mr Reynolds, these children have been up for over fifteen hours now.' Miss Roberts took Miss Evers' arm to try to stop her, but Miss Evers would go on. 'They have travelled nearly three hundred miles. You keep them waiting for another two hours or more and all you can say is you're sorry.'

Mr Reynolds looked down at Miss Evers. 'Lady, I've said I'm sorry. There's nothing more I can say if that won't satisfy you.' Then he looked up at the platform and walked towards the two boys who had stood up by this time. The dog followed and sat down by Mr Reynolds' feet, looking up at them.

'Sorry to keep you,' he said, looking from one to the other. He had bright blue eyes and the lines on his face disappeared into a beard that was flecked with white at the chin. There was wet mud down the front of his coat and David noticed a broad gold wedding ring on his hand as he ruffled the dog's neck. ''Twas the mare that did it. She foaled just half an hour ago, and I couldn't leave her. She had a bit of trouble, always does, this one. But we managed between us, and 'tis a good-looking foal, another colt though. Five foals she's had, and not a filly among them.'

'Filly?' said Tucky. 'What's that?'

'Horse, my dear,' and Mr Reynolds face creased into a smile. 'Filly's a girl horse. Colt's a boy, like yourself.'

'Mr Reynolds,' one of the village ladies came up beside him. 'Mr Reynolds, which one will you have?'

'Which one?'

'You put yourself down for one, Mr Reynolds. You said you only had room for one.'

'You want me to choose between these two boys, is that it?'

No one replied. He looked from David to Tucky and back again to David. ''Tis just like market day,' he said, shaking his head.

'Mr Reynolds!' Miss Evers stamped her foot in fury.

'This one's the fatter,' Mr Reynolds went on, looking at Tucky, 'but then this one's taller.' He reached out and gripped David's arm. 'He's a bit skinny, you know, not much meat on him.'

'Mr Reynolds, this is a serious matter,' said Miss Evers.

'You're right, lady, no doubt about it. 'Tis

a serious matter. I'm supposed to look at two young lads, face to face mind you, and then pick out one and not the other. Right enough, that's serious. 'Tis revolting that's what 'tis. And what happens to the one I don't choose, eh? How d'you think he'll feel?'

'As a matter of fact,' said Miss Roberts quickly, 'we don't know what will happen to him.'

'You don't know!'

'Apparently there's been a mistake, a muddle over numbers, and one of these two boys has nowhere to go, not yet anyway. I don't suppose you'd consider taking them both on, would you? They're great friends at school, and we'd be very obliged.'

'Friends, are they?' Mr Reynolds considered the two boys carefully and read each of their placards slowly, stroking his dog all the time. 'I'll tell you one thing for certain, it'll be both of them or neither. There'll be no choosing. What about asking them? They might not like the look of me – have you thought of that?' No one said anything, so he asked them direct. 'Well? What d'you think? I'm a farmer, forty-two years old, married, no children. My name's Jerry Reynolds, I run ninety-six acres – barley, sheep, milking cows, a few beef cattle and since the war began a few acres of potatoes. 'Tis only a small cottage, and you'll

29

have to share one bed and do your bit about the farm. Well? What d'you say?'

Tucky looked at David and David looked back at him. It was the first good moment of the day – each understood instinctively what the other wanted.

'We'll go with you, mister,' David said.

'Mr Reynolds, my dear, that's what you'll call me. And I'll be glad to have you both. Now take those things off from around your necks and get down here. You've given me a crick in my neck talking up at you like this.'

'Thank you, Mr Reynolds,' said Miss Roberts, shaking him by the hand. 'I've been their headmistress up till now, and they'll do you proud. You won't regret it.'

'I hope not,' Mr Reynolds said. 'Come on then you two, we'll be off. Haven't had my dinner yet. First the lambing then that confounded mare – quite put me out, it has.' The dog followed them towards the door.

'Mr Reynolds,' it was Miss Evers again. 'You must register before you take them.'

'Register?'

'It's regulations,' said Miss Evers icily. 'We have to know where the children are.'

'But you know that already, my dear,' Mr Reynolds smiled down at her. 'They'll be staying with us at Hamleigh Farm. Now you put that in your register, my dear. Goodnight to

30

you.' Anyone who put Miss Evers in her place was all right with David and Tucky.

It was cold outside and drizzling, and the boys pulled their coats around their legs inside the van and huddled together on the front seat. The van smelt like an animal, and as Mr Reynolds banged the door and got in beside them, they heard a rustle behind them. David twisted round in his seat and peered into the darkness.

'One of my orphan lambs,' said Mr Reynolds. 'Mother died this morning and I can't persuade any of the other ewes to take him on. He keeps warm in the back there – plenty of straw.'

'That dog,' said Tucky. 'Where's that dog?'

'Jip? He never comes in the car, doesn't trust it. He'll follow along behind – he always does.' The van started up with a rattle and a roar. 'Comfortable?'

'Yes thanks, mister,' said Tucky.

''Tis Mister Reynolds, Tucky. Can you remember that?'

3

The last leg of their journey was bumpy, noisy, smelly and draughty, but for David and Tucky it was the only enjoyable part of a long day. Now they were no longer going away, they were arriving. Every jolting minute was bringing them closer to a new home. They sat forward in their seat anxious for the first glimpse of the cottage, and then the thin beam of the headlights caught the glint of black windows ahead, and the car bumped off the road down a rough track and stopped.

Mr Reynolds clicked open the latch on the front door and had to bend his head as he went in. It was a long, low kitchen with a stove at one end and an oil lamp burning low on a table. It smelt of cooking and oil fumes. Mr Reynolds picked up the lamp and led them up a narrow, winding stairway.

'I told you you'd have to be in together,' he

said turning up the lamp. Shadows lightened and the room grew bigger. 'But there's good in everything. You'll be warmer this way. Your wash basin's on the chest, and there's a lavatory just outside the back door – through the kitchen. Don't forget to turn out the light before you go to sleep, will you?' He ruffled Tucky's hair and smiled broadly. 'You'll be all right then, my dears?'

'Mister . . . Mister Reynolds,' David corrected himself quickly. 'You said you were married, where's . . . ?'

'In bed, my dear. Ann's in bed. We get up with the light here and try to go to bed when it's dark – same way as the animals. You'll be seeing her in the morning.' He turned to go.

'G'night,' said Tucky.

'Goodnight to you both, and never you worry. Us'll be all right together.' The door closed.

David tried the water in the wash bowl with the tip of his finger, but that was all the washing he did. Tucky didn't even bother to do that. He had his pyjamas on in a flash and was in bed before David had started to undress.

Once in bed the two of them lay staring up at the bumpy ceiling.

'Wonder what's happening to the others,' said David.

'S'pose we'll be like brothers, you and me, kind of anyway.'

'Something like,' David muttered, wishing he'd kept his socks on like Tucky.

'I like that Mr Reynolds,' said Tucky and he pulled the quilt up tighter to his chin to shut out the cold air.

'Wonder what she's like, Mrs Reynolds; Ann he called her, didn't he?'

'Be all right if she's anything like him,' Tucky said.

'What, beard an' all?'

'Get off, didn't mean that,' Tucky giggled. 'Turn that lamp down, like he said. Here, listen. You can't hear anything, and you can't see anything. Can you hear anything Davey? Davey? . . . David?' But David was asleep, and before he had time to worry about it, so was Tucky.

In the morning it was the smell that woke them, and they dressed as if the house were on fire. They opened the kitchen door quietly. There was the sizzle and smell of frying eggs, and the thick gluey bubble of simmering porridge. Mrs Reynolds was bent over the kitchen stove with her back to them. She was small and slim and her dark hair was done up in a bun. The boys waited for her to turn and see them, neither of them wanting to make the first move. They stood transfixed by the smell until Mrs Reynolds turned with the saucepan of porridge in her hand.

'Morning, Mrs. I'm David and he's Tucky.'

David came further into the room. Mrs Reynolds' eyes widened in shock and they saw the porridge saucepan jolt in her hand. She looked from one to the other, and then put the saucepan down slowly. 'You frightened me for a moment. I thought you would still be in bed. I was going to call you when Jerry came in.' There was something different about her voice, and David noticed it immediately. Yesterday he had become used to the sing-song burr of the villagers. That was difficult enough to understand at times, and they did have some funny ways of putting things, but this was the halting accent of a foreigner. 'Of course, Jerry has told me about you. He said you looked like ghosts, no red in the face. And he was right too. A good hot breakfast and a day outside in the country air – that would be good for you, no? I am Ann, you must call me Ann, and you are David and Lucky.'

'Tucky,' said Tucky. 'It's Tucky. Tony Tucker, but everyone calls me Tucky.'

'Good. So you are Tucky and you are David. I'm right?' The boys nodded. 'Now, come and sit down at the table. Jerry will be in soon. He has to milk cows and feed the animals all before breakfast, you know.'

Breakfast lived up to expectations, and Ann fussed over them until they could eat no more. Just as they finished, Mr Reynolds came in.

'Feel better then, my dears? There's not a better cook in all England than my Ann. No doubt about that, no doubt at all.'

'My mum's good,' said Tucky.

'Course she is,' Mr Reynolds was pulling off his boots by the door. 'I forgot that. Let's say my Ann is the best cook in all Devon, and that with your mother Tucky and David's mother here the champion cooks of London, there's not a cook in the kingdom to touch them. Agreed?'

'Agreed,' said David, anxious to repair any offence Tucky might have caused. Tucky always said what he felt, and David was used to it by now.

Ann bustled over to Mr Reynolds now, prattling on happily in her strange accent. Everything about her was small, and next to Mr Reynolds she seemed even smaller and more delicate than she was. There was a gentleness in her eyes that was immediately comforting to David and Tucky; and whenever she smiled, and that was often, her whole face seemed to shine.

Tucky studied Mr Reynolds as he devoured his breakfast. 'Can I see that baby horse?' he asked suddenly.

'Baby horse! Baby horse!' Mr Reynolds roared with laughter. 'Did you hear the boy,

37

Ann? I told you, my dear, 'tis a foal, not a baby horse. A baby's a small one of us. Never make the mistake of thinking animals are like us. There's names for animals and names for us so that we can tell the difference. Animals are animals. You and me, Ann and Davey here – we're people, and that's different.'

'Baby horse or foal, Jerry,' Ann said, 'I think Tucky wants that he should see him.'

'And so he shall, Ann my dear, so shall they both, but after I've finished my breakfast – if they can wait that long.'

For David and Tucky it was worth waiting for. All that day and the next they saw things they'd never seen before as Mr Reynolds shepherded them around the farm. They watched him helping the foal born the night before, pulling him up on to wobbly legs. They discovered that the sheep on the steeply sloping fields were not wild after all; and the three milking cows, golden brown with white patches, wandered slowly towards them and did not attack. They watched Mr Reynolds delivering the early spring lambs, and helped him bring in the ewes that would be lambing soon. Then there were stakes to be driven in for fencing, water to be carried to the troughs in the fields and yards to be cleared. The two boys went everywhere with him, and Jip, the rangy black and white sheepdog, trailed along behind them.

By Sunday night David and Tucky knew their way round the farm and felt as if they'd been there for months. They felt at home. Neither of them had given Islington or home a thought. They had been too busy for that.

In bed that night the boys lay in the darkness, whispering.

'Which do you like best?' said Tucky.

'Can't say,' David whispered back after a long pause.

'I wish my dad was like him,' Tucky went on. 'I've never heard him shout, not like my dad. My dad's always on at me.'

'My father never shouted, not often anyway,' David tried to picture him shouting and couldn't.

'Can you remember your dad still?'

'Course I can. He was only killed a year ago. Year ago last month. Course I can remember him.'

'Bet you hate them after what they done to your dad. I would.'

'Course I do, everyone hates them.' And David tried to imagine his father's plane crashing on the beaches, as he'd done so many times before.

'I think she hates them too,' Tucky whispered.

'Who? Ann?'

'I asked her if Mr Reynolds was going to go away and fight, and she said he wouldn't be going. He's got to work the farm, and anyway he fought in the last war, wounded an' all. Then she asked me about my dad and I told her and then she asked all about you and your dad, so I told her. She went white as a sheet, honest she did. Didn't say anything, but she hates them, I can tell.'

'You shouldn't have told them. That's private, just between us,' said David.

'But she asked, Davey. I had to tell her, didn't I? Couldn't lie, could I?'

'School tomorrow,' David muttered. 'Be funny, all of us together in a different school, with different teachers. Wonder how all the others settled in. Wonder what the teachers will be like.'

'Can't be worse than Miss Evers,' said Tucky, and he tugged the quilt farther over his side. 'You keep pulling it over your side. I was frozen this morning when I woke up.' And David tugged it back and buried himself further down the bed.

Ann sent them off early the next morning for the walk to school. 'Not far short of three miles,' Mr Reynolds had said. 'You'll do it inside three parts of an hour, no question.' It seemed more like ten miles. Every bend brought another one and every hill a steeper one ahead. Jip came along with them, as far as the crossroads at the end of the lane, and then he stood looking after them, his tail drooping mournfully.

They ran the last half mile down into the village, their gas masks banging up and down on their backs. They had seen the village from the Reynolds' cottage. It stood on a hillside, a cluster of cottages with thatched roofs grouped under a tall grey church tower.

The village came upon them suddenly. They ran round a bend by a sign-post, and there was the school, just as Ann had explained. It was a long, low, gabled building built of purple-grey stone and grey tiles mottled with lichen. The playground outside was full – they were not late. Once inside the gate, they looked around for their friends from Islington and tried to ignore the inquisitive looks and huddled whispers of the village children.

'Where are they all?' said Tucky.

'P'raps they're late.' But the bell went as David was speaking.

The school was one big room on one floor with a great black boiler at one end, and two long rows of desks, the row at the back on a raised floor so that the children could all see the blackboard in front. There were only twenty or thirty children there, boys and girls.

Coats were hung up by the door and gas masks over the backs of the desks, and everyone sat down – everyone, that is, except

David and Tucky, who stood bemused by the door clutching their lunch boxes and gas masks.

At the far end of the room, beyond the boiler, a door opened, and there was a sudden and immediate silence as an old man walked slowly and deliberately towards the teacher's desk by the blackboard. As he sat down, all the children stood up and chanted in unison, 'Good morning, Mr Cooper'.

'Sit down,' the teacher said quietly. 'Good morning, children. The roll call please, Angela.'

'They got girls,' Tucky whispered. 'Do you think this is the right school?'

'Did you say something, lad?' The old man had swivelled round in his chair and was looking at them over the rims of his glasses.

'We were wondering, sir,' David said. 'We were told to come to school here, but none of our friends are here, so we thought perhaps we were in the wrong school.'

'You're David Carey and Tony Tucker?' They nodded. 'Then you're in the right place. In this school we always call the roll first before we do anything else. Do you understand?' He spoke clearly and kindly.

Angela called the roll, and each child stood up in turn, and then last of all she called out 'Tony Tucker', ' David Carey'. Mr Cooper then stood up and shook both of them by the hand.

'Welcome to our little school. I am the one and only teacher and my name is Mr Cooper, though no doubt the children call me something else. I require you to be polite, honest and hard-working. That is all. I hope you'll be very happy whilst you're with us.'

'What about all the others?' Tucky asked.

'Your friends from London have all gone to Imberleigh school. It's bigger there and there's more room.'

Mr Cooper turned to speak to the class. 'David and Tucky are evacuees, children. I told you we might be seeing new faces soon, didn't I? Well, here they are. I want you to remember that they are away from home, and that we are all very strange to them. We must all look after them and make them feel at home.'

Their welcome from the village children was cautious enough at first. But in morning playtime they were crowded into a corner under a big elm tree and bombarded with questions about London, about their homes, about German bombers. For a few days they felt they were the centre of attention. Whenever either of them spoke up in class everyone listened, and they were invited to eat their packed lunches at every house in the village. But it soon wore off, and within a few weeks they had been accepted as two 'townies' who were part of the village school.

There was a new pattern to their lives, broken only by letters from mothers, and the occasional glimpse of Miss Roberts in her hat whenever she came to the village. David's mother was stationed on an ack-ack battery on the south coast and wrote once a month. Tucky's parents were still in London but hardly ever wrote.

There was the walk to school after breakfast, usually in the rain; then morning prayers and the first lesson always with the gas masks on, when they all sat sweating and trying to concentrate on Mr Cooper's voice. Unless the sun was shining they took their packed lunches to a friend's house where there was always warm cocoa. After afternoon lessons there was the long walk home to the farm. Jip would meet them at the end of the lane by the crossroads, and they would race him home to tea with Ann in the smoky warmth of the kitchen. All that spring there were long walks on the moor that came down to where the farm ended. Mr Reynolds kept some sheep up there and the two boys came to know it well.

The war, London and Islington seemed to be in another world. Of course David looked forward to his mother's letter and kept every one under his pillow, and read and reread them whenever he could, but they seemed unreal.

There were signs a war was on. Mr Reynolds went off on Home Guard duty twice a week; there was a searchlight and an observation post in the village, and of course they still had their gas-mask drill. But there were no more bombs, and there was no more fear. They came to recognise Churchill's gruff voice over Mr Reynolds' crackling wireless set, and they noticed that Ann lost all laughter in her eyes whenever the war was mentioned. But it hardly ever was. Mr Reynolds used to say he was too busy to worry about the war.

Then one night in June the skyline of the moor was lit up with gun flashes, and a distant crump of bombing miles away on the other side of the moor brought the war back to David and Tucky and shattered their new-found peace.

4

David and Tucky watched from their bedroom window. The single beam of the searchlight from the village circled the sky above them, hesitating and retracing as it patterned the darkness.

They were alone in the house that night. Mr Reynolds had been called out on Home Guard duty, and Ann went up to the village with him to warm up the soup for them. It happened like that once a week and the boys were left to look after things on the farm.

'Like firework night,' said Tucky, resting his chin on his hands. And it was. There was the orange glow of fires, and the tracer for the anti-aircraft guns peppered the horizon with flashes and trails of hyphenated lights. They watched it as if it were a display. It was all a long way away, very different from the London raids they had both been through.

Here someone else was being bombed, not them.

'Tucky!' David whispered, grabbing his arm.

'What?'

'Listen! Can't you hear it?'

It was clear enough now, the deep throb of aircraft engines, punctuated by spluttering. They leaned farther out of the window and craned upwards, scanning the night sky. It came from over the moor, and they saw it at the same time, a red flicker first, and then three more lights floating down through the sky above the moor. But the throbbing and coughing had stopped now, and there was silence.

'The searchlight,' said David. 'Why doesn't it come this way? They'll miss it.'

But the searchlight was carving up the sky above the village at that moment, and the boys followed the lights as they fell lower and lower until they disappeared behind the moor.

'It's gone,' said Tucky. 'It's a German, wasn't it, Davey?'

'Crashed, must've crashed. It was going down all the time.'

'There'd have been a bang, an explosion or something.' Tucky pulled his head back inside.

'Could have landed,' David was thinking of

the flat valleys on the moor. 'Could have, you know. There's places where a plane could land out there.'

'In the dark? With no engines? Come on, Davey. It's gone behind a hill. That's all.'

'Then where is it, now, eh? Gone behind another hill? What goes down must come up. If it doesn't come up, it's crashed or it's landed; one or the other.'

Tucky saw the sense in that and they both kept watch, searching the darkness where the lights had vanished. And that's what they were doing when they heard Mr Reynolds' van splashing through the mud by the front gate.

Tucky was downstairs first and threw open the kitchen door. Ann was standing there, taking off her scarf.

'We saw a bomber, Ann. German bomber. We heard it and we saw it. There were lights, Ann, and Davey thinks it's gone down on the moor. There were lights, and they were coming down all the time, then they stopped. We saw it, honest we did, an' the engines were chugging and popping.'

'Tucky, Tucky,' Ann put an arm around him and brought him back into the light of the room. 'Don't be so excited, Tucky. How often do I tell you you must wear shoes on a stone floor? You catch cold that way.'

'What's up, Ann?' Mr Reynolds came in behind her.

'A plane's crashed,' said David simply, getting in before Tucky could start up again. 'It must've been one of the bombers.'

Mr Reynolds smiled. 'I been on searchlight all evening, my dear, and we saw them bombing around Plymouth, but we never saw a plane. No one saw a thing.'

'You missed it,' David said. 'It was out over the moor and your searchlight was up above the village.'

'Are you certain, Davey?' Mr Reynolds had stopped smiling now. ''Tis got to be for certain, y'know.'

'We heard, Mr Reynolds, honest we did,' Tucky said, feeling left out by now. 'It sounded just like the bombers used to sound in London. Just the same.'

Mr Reynolds and Ann looked at each other.

'And the engines were popping, just like Tucky says,' David could see they believed them now.

'Popping?' Ann said. 'What does it mean, this "popping"?'

'Must mean the plane had engine trouble of some sort,' said Mr Reynolds, looking from one boy to the other. 'Could've been hit. Was there any flames? Did you see any flames coming out of her?'

'Just the popping,' Tucky said. 'Then nothing and the lights went out.'

Mr Reynolds bent down and pulled the boys in towards him so that he could look into their faces. 'If there's been a plane down, I'll have to report it. There'll be the army and the police and they'll be wanting to ask you questions, lots of questions. Now think clearly, my dears. It must be for certain. Was there a plane?'

'We saw it, Mr Reynolds,' David said.

'And you're sure it came down over the moor?'

The boys nodded.

'It was there, Mr Reynolds,' said Tucky. 'I promise.'

'They're good boys, Jerry,' Ann said. 'They would not lie.'

'I know that, my dear,' said Mr Reynolds, standing up, 'but the army doesn't know that and neither do the police. They're the ones we'll have to convince. You did well to spot it my dears, and I'll be off back up the village to report it. There won't be much they can do till morning, and they'll be bound to want to see you then. So get off to bed with you both.' Ann went upstairs with them and they watched the glow of the fires on the horizon as Plymouth burned. She made them hot milk and sat on their bed while they drank it.

'It's a terrible thing they do,' she said sadly, gazing out of the window. 'When I was young I watched fires burning in my country, too. It's a terrible thing they do.' She spoke as the boys had never heard her before.

'You're not English, are you, Ann?' David had wanted to ask her that for a long time, but the moment had never been right.

'I'm French,' Ann said. 'I was French until I married Jerry. Now I am English like you; but I still think of France as my country. Like you, Davey, I know what it is to lose a father in war.' She took their mugs and left the room quickly.

'Now I know why she hates the Germans,' Tucky said quietly, as soon as her footsteps had reached the bottom of the stairs. And later when they were in bed Tucky could not help thinking about it. 'You're lucky.'

'Lucky?'

'If my dad was killed, I'd tell everyone. I'd be proud.'

'I am proud, Tucky. Ann's proud too, but it's better to have a father alive than be proud 'cos he's dead.'

'Depends on your father,' Tucky went on. 'And people like you if your father's dead, like you more anyway.'

'Do you like Ann more 'cos her father's dead?' David said. 'And me? What about me? We were friends years ago.'

'S'pose so,' said Tucky soulfully; and then he thought about the plane again. 'Davey, if that plane crashed like you said, then there'll be men on board. There'll be Germans. D'you think they'll find them?'

'I hope they're dead,' David said. 'They must've killed hundreds of people in Plymouth tonight. I hope they're dead. They deserve it.'

Neither of them slept much that night, and they heard Mr Reynolds coming back in his van some hours later. David thought of getting out of bed and asking about the plane, about what was being done, but he heard

Ann and Mr Reynolds talking together down in the kitchen and somehow he didn't want to see Ann again that night. Tucky got out of bed and tried to listen through the floorboards, but he couldn't make out what they were saying. Then a floorboard creaked and he scrambled back into bed.

It was still dark when Mr Reynolds woke them. He was in his Home Guard uniform. 'The army's downstairs. They want to be out on the moor by daybreak and they want you to come along and show them where it was, where you saw the plane. Quick as you can, my dears. We can't go till you're ready.'

The kitchen was full of uniforms, police and soldiers, and they all stood watching them eat down their porridge that Ann insisted they must have before they left. David looked up occasionally from his plate of steaming porridge and recognised some of the faces behind the uniforms. They looked tired and disbelieving. Mr Reynolds was bending over a map with a tall soldier in a peaked cap and a wet macintosh. ''Twas out of the bedroom window, sir,' he was saying, 'so it must be in this area here somewhere, almost for certain.'

'But Reynolds,' the officer took off his cap and shook it, 'there's two observation posts between here and there. Surely if there had been a plane someone else would have spotted it?'

'Not if they were following the searchlight, sir. The boys say the searchlight was sweeping over the village itself at the time.'

The officer turned to face the boys. He had a mean face with a thin moustache that barely covered his top lip. 'You say they're evacuees, Reynolds?'

'That's right, sir. And fine lads they are too, sir. Been with us for three months now. If they say they saw it, then you can be sure they did, sir.'

'Quite so, Reynolds,' said the officer, but he did not sound convinced.

Outside it was a drizzling grey dawn. There was a whole convoy of trucks blocking the lane, and the officer gave the order to get started. Ann wrapped them up in scarves and then they followed Mr Reynolds and clambered into the back of a jeep at the head of the column. The officer with the thin moustache clambered in front and nodded to his driver. 'I hope they're right, Reynolds. There's thirty Home Guard and a whole company from the barracks on this search. I hope you're right.'

David looked up nervously at Mr Reynolds who smiled and winked down at him. And Tucky was beginning to wish he'd never told anyone.

Ten times that day the convoy halted and the soldiers spread out over the moor and disappeared over the hilltops, their rifles hidden under their capes to protect them from the driving rain. The two boys were left behind with the trucks and drivers; and each time the soldiers came back empty-handed they felt worse. The officer kept asking them about the shape of the hills they had seen as the plane came down; he kept pointing up at the hillsides and asking them if they recognised the hilltop. But to the boys all the hills looked alike, and anyway they couldn't remember the hills from the night before, they hadn't even noticed the shape. The officer looked less and less pleased.

The rain cleared a bit after lunch and a spotter plane circled above them all afternoon. The soldiers, some of whom had been quite friendly to start with, now made little attempt to hide their feelings. It was clear what they thought of the 'townies' story.

For David and Tucky it was a nightmare. They knew there had been a plane, and they were almost certain it had come down; but each time a search failed and Mr Reynolds clambered wearily back into the jeep shaking his head, they began wondering if they had been seeing things that were not there.

By the time the convoy passed the cottage that evening and dropped them off, they knew that everyone thought they had invented the whole story. Even Mr Reynolds seemed dejected.

'Here you are,' said the officer as they jumped out. 'If it was a day off from school they wanted, Reynolds, then they certainly got it.'

'He didn't believe us,' said Tucky rather obviously as the trucks sped off up the lane.

'It's not your fault,' said Mr Reynolds, putting an arm round each of them. 'Maybe the plane wasn't as low as you thought, perhaps it managed to pull up.'

'We could have looked in the wrong places,' David said. 'The moor's a big place.'

'Course we could have, my dear,' said Mr Reynolds, ushering them in the door, 'but I don't think we did.' He didn't sound disbelieving or sarcastic, just weary.

'There was a plane, Mr Reynolds,' Tucky said as they were saying goodnight. 'We saw it, honest we did.'

'Course you did, Tucky. We both know you did, don't we Ann? Off you go now; it's been a long day, you're tired, I'm tired and Ann is certainly tired. She's done the farm all by herself today. Let's think no more about it.'

But they did think about it; they thought about little else all week. Everyone in the village had heard about the search and at school the 'townies' were not allowed to forget about it. Everyone had made up his mind: the 'townies' had got themselves off school for a day by calling out the Home Guard, the army and a spotter plane on some cock-and-bull story about a bomber coming down on the moor. Tucky was not the warlike type, but he very nearly got himself into a fight when someone suggested it might have been a flying saucer they'd seen and that they'd all better keep their eyes open for little men from Mars. Mr Cooper stopped it just in time, but none the less people laughed about it openly, and for the first time since they came to the village David and Tucky felt alone again and separate from the other children.

Time and time again they went over what they had seen that night, and time and time again they convinced themselves it had been a plane, that the engines had been spluttering and that it had been going down when the lights vanished. But every time they had to reconcile all that with the fact that no plane had been found, and all the reasoning in the world could not change that.

Ann tried hard to console them at home, explaining how easy it was to make mistakes, how often eyes could deceive.

'But we heard it as well, Ann. Both of us did,' said David.

Mr Reynolds stood up from the tea table and put on his hat. 'You still think there's a plane up there, don't you?'

'I know there is,' David replied.

'But we searched all day, Davey. There was nothing there.'

'Can't we try?' Tucky stood up. 'Can't we go and look for ourselves? I think we went too far away with the soldiers. It wasn't that far away. We heard those engines as if they were just over the cottage. I remember the windows shook.'

'Please, Mr Reynolds,' David added his support. 'Just one last chance, please.'

'All right, my dears, but I'll not be able to

come with you. I've left the farm for one day this week, and there's still a mass of work to catch up on. Farm doesn't work itself y'know and I can't leave it all to Ann now, can I?'

'It's Saturday tomorrow,' said Ann. 'It is lovely on the moor when it's fine, like it was today, and even if you don't find your plane, it would be a good walk anyway, no?'

'Only if it's fine, mind,' Mr Reynolds added, 'and you're not to go anywhere we haven't been together already. You'll have to turn around by midday. I don't want to call the army out again to come looking for you two on the moor. They may not be very keen to find you anyway.'

'Will they be safe, Jerry?' Ann looked worried.

'We've been up there often enough, I think. If the weather's right, they'll manage. I've told them and warned them often enough. 'Tis summer now, there's not much can go wrong if they stick to the tracks.'

It was fine again the next day, and the final search was on. It was still wet under foot as they tramped across the fields, but as soon as they reached the lower slopes of the moor, they felt the spring of the turf under their boots, and the higher they climbed the drier it became.

They navigated by following the line of the highest tor they could see from the bedroom window. The plane had vanished somewhere in line with that. 'Yes Tor' Mr Reynolds had called it.

Tucky was stronger and went on ahead, setting a fast pace, while David kept him going in the right direction from behind. They climbed rocky river valleys following the streams, but always when they had struggled up one valley there was another beyond, and Yes Tor seemed to have come no closer. At every hilltop they paused to catch their breath and search the vast emptiness of the moor. There were sheep enough, and they recognised the red mark of Hamleigh Farm they had marked Mr Reynolds' sheep with. Occasionally a group of sturdy brown ponies came in close to them but moved away as they approached them. But there was no aeroplane and no German pilots.

Sweaty and tired, they sat on top of a cairn eating the sandwiches Ann had made for them. The early optimism of the morning had gone, and the flies would not leave them alone. David looked at the watch Ann had lent him.

'After eleven already. An hour more and we'll have to give up and turn round.'

'Not worth going on,' said Tucky. 'We'll never find it, because it's not here. It never did crash. They're right, there's nothing here. Let's go back and forget about it.'

'One more hour, Tucky, that's all. Then we'll turn back, all right? We've come this far, we might as well finish it. There's a chance.' David was just as dejected as Tucky, but the thought of those children at school laughing at them next week, the thought of the look on their faces if they did find something – that was enough to drive him on.

At mid-day, under a blazing sun, having nothing but a few lizards in sight, they finally turned round and headed back towards the farm. Both of them had given up now, but David was still not going to admit it. As a matter of course they still searched the valleys and hills around them, but they were just retracing their steps and all hope had gone. They wanted only to get off the moor and forget the whole business.

As far as possible they followed the same tracks, but they took some short cuts as they trudged back down the hills, recognising landmarks ahead and making straight for them across country. On the way out they had kept close to the paths Mr Reynolds had shown them, but on the way back nothing seemed to matter any more and they just wanted the quickest route home.

David was leading by now, and Tucky trailed behind him, dispirited and silent. But it was Tucky who suggested that instead of following the river to the stepping stones at the foot of the valley, they might as well cross higher up and cut off over the moor.

Tucky was first in the water, holding his boots and socks up above his head. 'S'easy,' he said. 'Come on, you can do it.'

'Too fast for me,' said David, watching the water foaming furiously round Tucky's legs. 'I'll go on down to the stepping stones and cross there, like before.' David wasn't scared, it was just a feeling that the water looked too fast as it whipped round the rocks. Tucky was jumping from stone to stone, and when he got to the middle he turned round and waited for David to join him. David managed it to the middle and they stood on the rock and looked at the gap they had to jump.

'I'll go first,' Tucky shouted over the roar of the water. The gap yawned wide, frothing and swirling, but Tucky leapt and landed easily enough on the plateau of rock on the other side. He turned, balancing precariously, and beckoned David. David screwed himself up for the jump, trying not to look down into the water.

'Jump upwards,' he said to himself. Once he nearly went but he held back at the last moment.

'Come on, Davey. You can do it. Just jump.'

David took a deep breath and jumped, but his foot slipped behind him on the rock and he fell forward into the water. He heard Tucky

shouting, and looked up to see his outstretched hand. His feet struck out in panic
and the water pulled him away. His fingers
reached out for the rock above him, but then
the water closed in over him and he was dragged irresistibly downwards. He tried to cough
the water out of his lungs, but more was
coming in all the time and he couldn't seem
to do it. He came up once into the brightness
of the sun and Tucky was running along the
bank screaming something at him. Then the
water whisked him round, his back thudded

into a rock and he was underwater again, and his boots seemed heavy.

Then he remembered he could not swim, and it came to him coldly that if he could not swim, then he would drown. He screamed in his terror and the water poured into his mouth cutting him short. The more he kicked the deeper down he went. He came up again, arms flailing. Tucky was standing there watching, his mouth wide open.

An arm was around his neck and another under his shoulders, and he was being dragged back against the force of the water. He struggled, but the grip tightened fiercely and he was pushed under the water. I'm drowning, he thought, and Tucky's just standing there. He can swim, I've seen him at Birchington. Why doesn't he help me? Why doesn't Tucky help?

5

The sun was dazzling his eyes and Tucky was leaning over him. From somewhere there was the smell of wood smoke.

'Davey! Davey! Can you hear me? You all right?' Tucky seemed to be shouting, but David heard him only faintly at first. 'We were right, Davey. It *was* a bomber, a German bomber, and there's two of them here.'

'Two?'

'Two German pilots. One's hurt but the other one pulled you out of the river.'

David pushed himself up slowly and propped himself on his elbows. The smoke came from a fire a few feet away, and beyond that up against a low dry stone wall there

were two men in blue uniforms. One of them stood up now and came towards them. There was the black butt of a revolver sticking out of his belt, and David saw that he was unshaven. He was wearing only a shirt and trousers and they were clinging wet. He crouched down a few paces away.

'Your friend is well now?' He spoke haltingly, with a heavy accent. 'He is better?'

'You tell him, mister,' Tucky said excitedly. 'You tell him. You're a German, aren't you?'

The man nodded. 'We are German, yes.'

'See, Davey. There was a plane and it did crash.'

'You were in that plane?' David was trying to take it all in.

'It was my plane, yes. We were hit and then we lost power. We had to crash-land.' His eyes were sunk deep in his head, and his hair was still wet.

'You were bombing Plymouth?' David asked. He could feel a knot of anger building up inside him. The man nodded slowly.

'Their plane sank,' Tucky went on. 'That's what he told me. Landed in a bog. Remember Mr Reynolds telling us that story of a horse and rider that were sucked down – that's what happened to their plane. That's what he said.'

'And they've been out here all week?' David said, looking past the fire to the man by the wall.

'S'pose so,' said Tucky. 'That one's hurt his leg or something, doesn't speak any English.'

David looked at them both. There was nothing threatening or frightening about them, they were just two exhausted, pale-looking men with sad eyes and kind faces. They were faces he should hate. Perhaps these were the men who had shot down his father over the French coast and cheered as they watched him crashing into the beaches. These were the men who had bombed London and Plymouth and killed thousands. Yet one of them had saved his life.

'He took your clothes off, Davey, after he dragged you out. They're over there by the fire. Should be dry soon, you were unconscious long enough.' David had been aware of a roughness against his skin, but it was only now that he realised he was covered in a dark blue overcoat. His clothes were hanging over a frame of sticks by the fire.

'My friend is not well,' the German said. 'He cannot move much and he is cold. I need food – food and blankets. The nights are cold here and he coughs. Will you help us, please?'

'Help you!' David was almost shouting. He pulled himself to his feet, gathering the great-coat around him. 'Help you? After what you've done? You come here bombing and killing and you want us to help you!'

'It is a war,' he replied sadly. 'In war people die – on both sides.'

'Why don't you give yourself up?' Tucky said. 'You can't escape, not if your friend can't move. And there are soldiers out looking for you, you know. We told them about your plane.'

The German threw more wood on the fire. 'Perhaps you are right,' he said, 'but we must try. We need time to recover. Two days ago we have finished the emergency food. We have nothing left – just water from the river. This is the first fire I have dared to light. We must keep warm, and we must have food. Then we will escape over the moor to the sea and find a boat.'

'What about the soldiers?' said Tucky.

'They did not find us last time. It is a big place to search, this moor.'

'And what if we tell them where you are?' David said, as defiantly as he could.

'Then we shall be caught, my young friend. I cannot move my friend any more now, and I cannot leave him. We are in your hands,' and he turned away and walked back to his friend on the other side of the fire.

'What do we do?' Tucky whispered. 'We got to help him, haven't we? He saved your life, Davey, pushed all the water out of you and he was risking a lot to light that fire for you. You owe him, Davey. We both do.'

saving your life, then I think it's a pity he went in after you.'

David had never heard Tucky like this. He was excitable, yes; impetuous, yes; but he'd never found him determined or single-minded.

Tucky leaned towards him over the kitchen table. 'I like you, Davey. We've been best friends ever since I can remember. You always seemed to do right by people. You've done right by me, been a real friend since we left home, but if you turn those Germans in just because your father . . .'

'My father?'

'That's what it is, Davey, isn't it? And maybe Ann's father as well. They're Germans and the Germans killed your dad, so you hate them all, don't you, every one of them?'

There was not a single word Tucky had spoken that David could argue with. Tucky was right. He did owe the Germans out on the moor.

'All right,' he conceded. 'We'll do it, but not for long.'

Tucky smiled like his old self for the first time since they had got back. They didn't see Mr Reynolds again that evening; he was busy fencing at the bottom of Front Meadow. But next morning over breakfast, before David and Tucky left for school, he heard all about their search on the moor. 'So, you found nothing,' he smiled wryly, 'and Davey here fell in the river.'

'I slipped, Mr Reynolds. Those stones were all slimy.'

'You crossed at the stepping stones, like I said?'

'Yes, Mr Reynolds.'

'And no sign of that plane?'

'Nothing,' said Tucky. 'We must have made a mistake. P'raps it went up again, behind a hill or something, and we just didn't see it. Sorry, Mr Reynolds.'

'Never you mind, my dear. You were right to tell us if you thought you saw it. Everyone makes mistakes, and anyway 'twas good practice for the army and for us – even if no one enjoyed it much. We won't mention it again. Off you go now, you'll be late for school.'

School was still buzzing with the 'townies' shot-down German bomber, and David and Tucky longed to blurt out their secret. 'Haven't you found it yet, Davey boy?' and 'Look out, the Luftwaffe's about!' And whenever Mr Cooper wanted someone with a good imagination, he turned to the 'townies' with a knowing smile, and everyone laughed.

It was a wretched day, only made bearable by the knowledge that they knew they were right. On the way back home that afternoon, they worked out their plan.

'Whatever happens, Mr Reynolds and Ann

must never find out. Never,' said David. 'Nothing must be missed.'

'What about the blankets? They'll miss those, won't they? They're bound to.'

'Not if we take two off our bed,' said David. 'We make our own beds, don't we? No one'll miss them, 'cept us. We can bring them back after they've gone. No one need notice.'

'What about the food then?'

'There's eggs,' David had thought it all out. 'We can get them from the chicken hut soon as we get back. Then there's carrots and radishes in the vegetable patch – I've seen Ann pulling them up often enough. I know where they are.'

'That won't be enough.'

'Then there's that bowl of bread and leftovers that Ann keeps on the window ledge above the sink. We could take that, some of it anyway. No one would miss that – 'cept the pigs, of course.'

David had been planning it all day, and once they got home, he knew exactly what had to be done. He sent Tucky upstairs for the blankets while he went for the food. As he expected, Ann was out with Mr Reynolds haymaking across the stream by Long Close; it was far enough away from the house for it to be safe. They wrapped the food in one of the blankets and made off out of the back door, and across the fields towards the moors.

Once off the farm they kept to the cover of the hedgerows until they reached the open moor and were out of sight of the cottage. Tucky flopped down behind a stone wall and waited for David to join him. He fought to catch his breath, hanging his head back and taking in great gulps of air. David slumped down next to him and checked that the food was still inside the blankets. One egg had broken, but everything was there. It was then they heard someone coming up the track behind them. They looked at each other in alarm. The panting was close now, just the other side of the stone wall. They froze against it, rigid and frightened. And then Jip came lolloping into sight, saw them cowering there and trotted over, tail wagging, tongue hanging down from his pink and grinning mouth. They laughed themselves silly with relief.

'Dogs can't tell tales,' David said, and Jip followed them along over the hills to where the river tumbled over the rocks. They crossed over the stepping stones and clambered on up, always looking ahead of them to see if the Germans were still there. They approached the place slowly, but Jip ran on ahead sniffing the ground busily, alternately growling and yapping in his excitement. He disappeared behind the stone wall, and then there was silence.

The German airmen were where they had left them, only closer in among the rocks. One of them held Jip under his arm, his hand clamped over his muzzle. Both wore their blue greatcoats and were crouching down low. Their faces relaxed and the black revolver that was pointing at the boys was lowered.

'Is it your dog?' he asked. David nodded, and the German released Jip and patted his neck gently. Jip sprang away and cowered behind the boys. 'Food? Have you brought food?' David handed over the blanket, and the two Germans spread it out carefully in front of them. They divided it equally and then devoured it like starved dogs, looking up from time to time as if someone might take it away from them.

The boys looked on in silence, wondering how anyone could be that hungry. They ate anything and everything – meat fat, cold porridge, stale bread, peelings, carrots, raw eggs. When they had finished not a crumb was left on the blanket – except the eggshells. They sat back against the wall, breathing deeply.

'That was good, very good,' the airman was panting. 'Gurt here, he slept hardly at all, it will be good for him. You are kind, very kind. Thank you, it was a feast, a real feast.'

The boys saw that the men had built themselves a rough shelter up against the wall since the day before. It was made of wooden

supports, and covered in bracken, dried grass and freshly cut turf. There was more bracken on the floor inside and enough room for both men to squeeze in together. 'It's not a palace, my young friend,' he said, 'but it is better than nothing.' The German smiled quietly as he spoke, but then his face altered suddenly.

They all heard it together, the drone of an aeroplane, and it was coming closer all the time. The two Germans crawled in under their shelter and pulled the blankets in after them. Tucky spotted it first as it came over the hill, a single-engined spotter plane, a biplane, and it flew down towards them over the moor, its RAF markings plainly visible. It was the same spotter plane that had been used in the search the week before.

6

'Wave,' David shouted. 'Wave at him.' And Tucky obeyed instinctively, waving after the plane as it banked and came in for a second run. David gave the thumbs-up sign and the 'V' for victory. 'Look happy, Tucky, smile at him.'

The spotter plane swept down even lower this time, and they could see the pilot waving back at them, and the two boys waved after it as it waggled its wings in salute. Tucky glanced down at the Germans' shelter, but there was no sign of them, and by the time he looked up again, the plane was climbing fast over the moor and turning towards the south.

'What if they saw?' Tucky tugged at David's elbow. 'What if they saw the Germans?'

'They didn't, they couldn't have.' David was almost sure. 'We're two boys out with our dog on the moor, nothing wrong in that, is there?'

'And that shelter, what about the shelter?'

David didn't have the time to answer. 'So, you told them about us.' The boys swung round at the sound of the German's voice. He was standing up by the shelter, his greatcoat pulled up under his chin.

'No, mister, we didn't tell no one. Honest.' Tucky sounded frightened.

'Honest?' He came towards them. 'And the plane? The plane was not sent. You told no one?'

'No one,' said David firmly, moving closer to Tucky. 'We kept it a secret. I didn't want to, but he did, and we told no one.'

'But you were waving,' the airman went on. 'You wanted them to see you, to see us.'

David shook his head. 'Do you think we'd want to be caught giving food and blankets to Germans? Do you? We were waving to show them we weren't in any trouble. That's all.'

He looked hard at both of them, and then went back to the shelter to talk with his friend who had crawled out by now. For some minutes they talked agitatedly in German, and the boys stood and waited. Finally he came back towards them.

'You are right,' he said. 'I am sorry it is like this for you. My friend, Gurt, he says we should trust you. He says you have already done enough to pay me for yesterday. He says we should not ask you to help your country's enemies. You would have trouble if you were caught, no?' David nodded. 'We just ask you one more thing. Then no more. Tomorrow we will try to cross the moor to the sea. My friend is no better. His cough is worse, and his leg is not good, but we must try. We need one more day to gain our strength. We need one more good meal, and some drink – brandy perhaps, to keep us warm inside. Can you do this for us?'

David and Tucky looked at each other. 'This'll be the last?' said David. 'There'll be no more?'

'You have my word. It is the last.'

'All right, mister. We got to go now. We'll be back this time tomorrow,' and David whistled for Jip who was sniffing the blankets. 'Come on, Jip.'

'Thank you again, my friends,' the German said, and his friend by the shelter smiled weakly and waved his thanks.

The boys were at the bottom of the valley before either of them spoke, and Jip was running on ahead chasing every scent he found. 'Not so bad, are they Davey? For Germans, I mean?'

'Brandy,' David muttered. 'And where do they think we're going to get brandy from?'

'There's some bottles under the stairs,' said Tucky. 'Where Mr Reynolds gets his cider from.'

'Steal them, you mean. We've got to steal from Ann and Mr Reynolds?'

'We stole the eggs, didn't we?' said Tucky.

'That's different,' said David, and he felt uncomfortable as he said it.

Mr Reynolds was out on Home Guard duty again by the time they got back, and they helped Ann feed the stock and shut them up for the night. 'Not many eggs,' Ann said as they were crossing the yard. David and Tucky said nothing. 'Twice as many yesterday, something must have frightened them. Jerry said there might be a fox about. And I left the bowl of slops for the pigs on the ledge above the sink – just like always. You did not move it, did you boys?'

'Probably Jip,' David said quickly. 'He's always at the dustbins and things. He's taken them before, hasn't he?'

'Strange, though,' Ann went on.

'What is?' Tucky was nervous, and he showed it.

'You could be right, Jip does take the slops sometimes, but he doesn't put the bowl back on the kitchen table when he has finished.'

'That yellow bowl?' David asked. 'I found it outside in the yard, Ann. It was upside down by the trough, so I put it back in the

kitchen.' David hadn't the courage to look at Ann as he spoke. She seemed happy with his explanation, and forgot all about it. But at supper she reminded Jerry about the fox. 'I think it must be that, Jerry. They are not laying away, and they're eating as good as ever. Must be the fox.'

Mr Reynolds was still in his uniform, and unbuttoned his tunic. 'Course it could be, but 'tis the early spring they come after the fowls, when there's cubs to feed. 'Tis a bit late now, and I haven't seen him about for weeks. The old fox, he's a cunning old devil. He doesn't come after the fowls on a bright summer's day; he waits till the wind's up high, and comes around dusk. That's when you want to watch out for the fox. Old devil, he is. No, they've just gone off the lay – they do it from time to time. Get a bit lazy, just the same as we do.' He sniffed the air greedily and rubbed his hands. 'That smells good enough, Ann my dear.'

'I made that potato pie with eggs, but there will not be enough egg, not as much as there should be.'

Mr Reynolds leaned up against the cooking stove and warmed his hands on the pipes. ''Tis the coldest place on God's earth, that moor. Even in high summer, the evenings are like winter. 'Tis terrible. Still 'twas a good exercise, very good.'

'Up on the moor?' David's heart seemed to come up in his mouth.

''Twas after our little caper last week, my dear, the good Captain thought we should have more practice at searching up there. So up we went – and 'twas a good thing we did, too.'

'What d'you mean?' David thought he would choke on his mouthful.

'Did you find anything?' Tucky asked, all the colour drained from his face.

'Course we did. If the Home Guard goes out on a search, you can be sure they find something.'

'What did you find, Jerry? Don't keep on. You're teasing,' said Ann, laughing.

'No planes, my dears, no Germans, I'm afraid, just two of my sheep stuck fast in a bog.' Mr Reynolds' face wrinkled into a smile. 'Poor little devils, been like that all day by the state of them; right up over their backs it was. You'd think the sheep would know where to go and where not to go, wouldn't you?' The boys laughed with Ann, in a desperate attempt to hide their relief.

Once in bed that night, the boys lay still, listening to the talk downstairs, listening for any sign that Ann or Mr Reynolds was suspicious.

'Do you think they know?' Tucky whispered.

'Not yet. Don't think so.'

'I saw those bottles under the stairs like I said. There's loads of them, Davey. They won't notice if one's missing.'

'Won't they?' David was sullen.

'When shall we take one?' Tucky shifted up on his elbow.

'Why don't you go and ask them if you're in such a hurry?' David snapped angrily. 'Why don't you go down and tell them we're looking after two Germans on the moor, and would they mind if we took a bottle of brandy to keep them warm and help them to escape.'

Tucky was silent for a moment. 'No need to have a go at me, Davey.'

'Well, it was your idea, wasn't it?' David hissed.

'S'pose so.' Tucky lay down again. 'But we had to do it, Davey. We got to do it.'

'Why?'

''Cos we said we would, that's why.'

'And Ann and Mr Reynolds. Have you thought what we're going to say if they find out what we've done? What are we going to tell them, Tucky?'

'I dunno,' said Tucky. 'I hope they never find out, 'cos I dunno.'

School was slow the next day. Every lesson dragged on, and it seemed as if the last bell would never ring. For Tucky it was spent wondering about the two airmen up on the moor, hoping no one else would discover them, and speculating whether or not they'd make it to the sea. David could think of nothing but the brandy, about how he was going to steal from two of the best people in the world to help the same people who had killed his father. He hated what he was doing, and dreaded having to do it.

Ann and Mr Reynolds were out turning the hay as they came back up the lane. Mr Reynolds was waving his rake, calling to them to come over. He was leaning up against the cart wiping the sweat away from his eyes. 'Got a job for you two,' he said. 'Jip's gone off, my dears. I was up on the moor this morning turning out the late lambs and Jip took it in his head to run off. I nearly went after him, but while the weather's right I thought I'd best get on with this. Course he'll find his way back himself like as not, but I'd be happier if you'd go out and find him. He made off in the direction of the river I think.' He stopped and looked closely at David. 'What's the matter, Davey? You don't look too good.'

'Nothing,' said David hurriedly.

'We'll find him, Mr Reynolds,' said Tucky. 'We were going up on the moor anyway, weren't we, Davey?'

'Don't be late for supper,' Ann called after them.

They ran back to the cottage first and dropped their school things in the bedroom. Tucky pulled off his pillowcase. 'We can use this to carry the food,' he said.

'You know where Jip went, don't you, Tucky? He went off to see them. What if Mr Reynolds had followed him? They've got a gun, haven't they?'

'They'd never use it, would they?' Tucky

said. 'They never used it on us. They're not like that. They wouldn't have hurt him, and anyway, it never happened. Stop worrying about it. Come on.'

Tucky was impatient to get out there and he went off in search of food with strict instructions from David to take nothing that would be missed. David made sure Ann and Mr Reynolds were still out in the field and then went downstairs to find the brandy. He sorted through the bottles under the stairs, looking over his shoulder every few seconds to make sure no one was coming. He felt like a thief in the night. There was no brandy, only a bottle of whisky, half full, and crates and crates of empties. He took the whisky and tucked it under his shirt.

They met at the door and ran, Tucky holding the pillowcase in front of him and David clutching the whisky in both hands as he tried to keep up with Tucky. They reached the stone wall again, and flopped down behind it.

'Look,' Tucky panted, opening up the pillowcase. 'Look what I got.' There were eggs again, two tins of corned beef and the remains of the pie from the evening before.

'You're mad, Tucky, why d'you take that?'

'That's all there was, honest. There were masses of tins like this and I left some of the pie in the bowl. There was nothing in the slops bowl. S'all I could find, Davey.'

It was clouding over now, and the hills on the moor were changing colour. The stones took on a deeper granite grey, and the grass turned almost purple on the hillsides. As they clambered up the hill towards the Germans' hide they felt the first drop of rain. But this time they felt something was wrong. It was all too quiet. They called out for Jip, but there was no answering bark.

The hide was deserted, the shelter had disappeared as if it had never been there. Only the damp grey ashes by the stone wall were left to show that anyone had been there at all.

7

The boys stood in the drizzle calling and whis-
tling for Jip, and then from high up on the
hills came a familiar barking. It seemed to be
coming from the cairn, a massive pile of
granite rocks that dominated the valley like
some prehistoric fortress. Tucky whistled
again, and back came Jip's reassuring bark;
and then they saw him standing up on the
cairn against the sky, his body shaking as he
barked. Tucky set off up the hill with David
in close pursuit; and Jip jumped down from
the rocks and bounced down towards them,
tail bobbing, tongue hanging out.

It was a long climb up. They had to make
frequent detours to find the safest way to the
top, zigzagging up the hill towards the cairn.
Jip could climb where they could not and ran
on ahead, turning every so often to make sure
they were following.

Tucky stopped to catch his breath and

shouted up, 'You up there? We got your food.' For some moments there was no response.

'Come up.' It was the German's voice from behind the rocks. There was no doubt about that. Tucky waited for David and they went on up together.

It was a small grassy clearing encircled by great boulders, and in one corner a great granite slab had fallen across the walls to form a roof. It reminded David of pictures he'd seen of Stonehenge, only smaller. One German was lying down under the roof, covered in blankets, and the other stood beside him stroking Jip.

'We thought you'd gone,' Tucky said. 'You didn't tell us you were moving.'

'The plane that came over yesterday,' he said. 'I thought it could have seen us. It was a good thing. There were soldiers out yesterday, just the other side of the river. We are safe here now.'

David was looking at the other airman, who was struggling to sit up. 'Your friend? Is he worse?'

'Not good, not good. He is very ill. You have brought the brandy?'

'Whisky,' said David. 'There was no brandy.' He handed him the bottle.

'Thank you, my friend,' the German's face broke into a half smile. 'It will be a help.' He was even paler than the day before, and his beard had grown darker. He knelt down beside his friend and helped him to sit up. He tilted the bottle and the boys watched the injured German drink it as if it was water. Twice his whole body was shaken by violent coughing fits, but still he came back for more until finally he pushed it away. He leant back against the rocks, nodded at the two boys and smiled his thanks. Tucky put the pillowcase down inside the shelter and stood back.

'We won't bring any more,' David said suddenly when they had finished emptying the pillowcase. They ate on as if he had said nothing, ripping open the tins of corned beef and shovelling the meat directly from the tins into their mouths. David said it louder. 'We have done enough. There won't be any more. You understand?'

The German nodded as he finished his mouthful and wiped his mouth with the back of his sleeve. 'You have done more than enough. It is good that we can help each other in these sad times. It is good.'

'We only did it 'cos you helped us,' David said. 'That's all. We're still enemies.'

'No, I don't think so,' he looked up at them and smiled. 'I am wearing the uniform of your enemy, but we are not enemies, not any more.'

'We must take Jip now,' David said, wanting it to be over. 'We were sent out to find Jip. We've got to get back.'

The airman got to his feet slowly, holding out his hand to stop them. 'Please,' he said, 'there is one last thing.'

'No,' David was almost shouting. 'It's finished. I've paid you back, haven't I? We won't do any more, do you understand? No more.'

'Please.' The German took a step closer, and the boys backed away. 'We want no more food, no more anything.'

'Come on, Tucky.' David turned to go. 'I'm going.'

'I want you to take my friend back with you,' said the German quietly. 'As your prisoner. He has agreed. He is not well enough to go with me over the moor. I hoped food and warmth would help, but it hasn't. He wishes to go with you as your prisoner.'

'You want us to take him? Hand him over to the army?' Tucky said. Pictures of him leading a captured German pilot through the village, with crowds cheering and church bells pealing, came swarming into his mind. Their faces! The look on their faces!

'How far is it?' the German asked.

'How far?' David was still trying to take it in.

'To your home, your village?'

'It's not our home exactly,' he said. 'We're evacuees.'

'From London, mister, to get away from the bombs,' Tucky answered for him.

The man nodded knowingly, and looked hard at David. 'From London. I am sorry, my friends. Perhaps when you are older you will understand that we all do things we know we should not do. But perhaps you have learnt that already.'

David looked away. 'It takes over an hour,' he said. 'But it's downhill most of the way.'

'To begin with I will go with you – Gurt, my friend, he cannot walk too far – I will come to help carry him. He is a big man, too heavy for you, I think. You will take him?'

'We will, won't we Davey?' Tucky was eager.

'All right,' David said. 'But no one must see you. You won't make it, you know.'

'Make it?'

'Over the moor. It's thirty miles of hills, bogs and rivers, and the army trains all over it. They'll catch you, and if they don't, the moor will kill you.'

'Will you tell them about me?'

David shook his head. 'There's no need. Mr Reynolds says no one can cross the moor from north to south without a map or a compass, and without knowing the moor. You'll never do it.'

'In planes we navigate by the stars,' he said. 'The moor may be big, but it is not as big as the sky. I will try anyway. I have to try. If you were away from home, and you wanted to get back, you would try, wouldn't you?'

They started off down the hill, Jip prancing on ahead sniffing at every rabbit hole. Tucky carried both the blankets over his shoulder, and kept looking round every few yards to make sure the two Germans were still behind them. David stuffed the pillowcase inside his jumper and wondered how they were going to explain away the blankets to Mr Reynolds. The deception was getting too complicated; something must go wrong, he was sure of it.

The boys found themselves walking too fast for the airmen, who needed to stop to rest from time to time. The injured one was being carried, slung over his friend's shoulder in a fireman's lift. David and Tucky sat down on a rock to wait for them to catch up. It was still drizzling and the German found it difficult to keep his feet as he came down towards them. He plodded on past them, and David saw the effort on his face and a look of grim determination.

'What're we going to say?'

David had made up his mind. 'We bumped into them by accident. No need to lie any more, Tucky.'

'That's just it,' Tucky went on. 'There's two

of them, and we're only bringing one of them in. What're you going to do about the other one? Are we going to tell them or what?'

'I don't know.' David got up and followed the Germans.

David stopped them when they reached the low stone wall that separated the moor from the farm, and here the airman lowered his friend gently on to his feet. They talked to each other briefly in German, and then shook hands solemnly.

'You will look after him, please?' he said. 'He needs a doctor. You will make sure he has a doctor?'

'Course we will,' Tucky said excitedly. 'Course we will, won't we, Davey?' And David nodded his agreement.

'So, he is your prisoner now,' and he felt deep into the inside of his coat and pulled out the black revolver. 'You will need this,' he said, handing it to David. It was cold and heavy, heavier than David had imagined. 'It is loaded, but the safety catch is on. Be careful with it, please.' David balanced it in his hand and gripped the butt, his finger curling round the trigger.

'I could make you come too,' he said.

'Of course, Davey.' The man nodded. 'But friends do not use guns on each other.' He held out his hand to David. David looked down at the outstretched hand and took it.

'Goodbye, Davey, and you too, Tucky, Auf Wiedersehen.'

''Bye,' said David.

'And good luck,' Tucky shouted after him. But the German was striding away into the rain, head bent forward, the collar of his coat turned up to cover his neck.

Mr Reynolds was in the yard, bringing in the sows. He heard footsteps behind him, and then Jip was nuzzling his leg. 'So you little devil, you. You found him then, my dears.' He still had not turned round. 'Dogs are like horses, got minds of their own.'

'We found him, Mr Reynolds,' said Tucky. 'And someone else. Look.'

Mr Reynolds turned and stared. 'Your plane? From your plane, is he?' he could hardly believe what he was looking at.

'Jip found him, Mr Reynolds,' said David. 'He's a German bomber pilot – Luftwaffe.'

'I can see that, my dear, I can see that.' He looked the German up and down, and then he noticed the revolver David was holding in his hand. 'Now, you give that thing to me, my dear,' he said, and he walked round the German, keeping his distance, and took the revolver from David. 'Ann,' he called out, not taking his eyes off the German. 'Ann, come here. Come out here.' He was pointing the

100

revolver at the German now and waving him towards the cottage.

'Your plane, must've been your plane, 'most for certain. You were right, my dears, right after all. Does he speak English?'

'No,' Tucky said. He was longing to see Ann's face when she saw.

'He's limping, isn't he? Course he's been out on the moor for the best part of a week; no, 'twould be more now, wouldn't it? Looks half starved, doesn't he? Ann!'

Ann threw open the door and came running out, her hands white with flour. She stopped dead and her hand shot to her mouth.

'German pilot,' Tucky said. 'From our plane. We found him out on the moor.'

'Jip found him,' David said quickly.

'Did he hurt you?' Ann had gone white.

'Gentle as a lamb, by the look of him,' said Mr Reynolds.

'But the gun,' said Ann. 'The gun. How did you get the gun?'

'Just gave himself up,' David said. 'He can hardly walk, Ann; he's tired out and coughing; he should see a doctor.'

'The van, my dear, get the van out,' said Mr Reynolds. 'Take it up to the village and get Captain Starey, and if he's not there, then ring up the army at Okehampton. They'll send someone out, but quick as you can now.

We'll look after him here, won't we, my dears?'

Ann came closer to the German and looked up into his face. 'Just people, just ordinary people, like you and me,' she said.

In the warmth of the kitchen the German sat in Ann's chair by the stove, holding a mug of tea in his hands, and shivering. Mr Reynolds nursed the revolver, shaking his head.

'And the blankets, I don't understand about the blankets,' he said slowly. 'They're ours, no doubt about that. That green one, I've seen that one on my bed before now, most for certain. 'Twas on my bed for years.'

'We found all sorts up there,' David spoke up confidently. 'We brought them all back, the blankets, a bottle of whisky and this pillow-case. He must've taken them, come here and taken them.' David had thought it all out as they came across the fields, and the story came out now convincingly. Mr Reynolds nodded thoughtfully, but said nothing.

'And the plane?' he asked. 'No sign of that plane, I suppose.'

'We looked all around – there was nothing, not a sign.'

'Crashed into a bog,' Tucky blurted out, and David winced. They had agreed David would be the spokesman, that Tucky would keep quiet.

'How do you know that, my dear?' Mr Reynolds looked up sharply. 'He couldn't have told you, he doesn't speak English, does he?'

'He doesn't know, not really,' David said, willing Tucky to keep his mouth shut. 'Tucky's just guessing, that's all. Don't see what else could have happened though. We reckoned it must've crashed and then sank in a bog – that's what we thought anyway.'

'Ah,' Mr Reynolds nodded. 'There is that, I suppose. 'Tis a possibility, no doubt. And did you see any sign of anyone else up there, Germans, I mean? I was thinking that there's more than one man in a bomber crew, and it was a bomber wasn't it?' David nodded. The question was too close, and Mr Reynolds was talking strangely. He was suspicious; David was sure of it. 'Now there's as many as six or eight in one of their bombers, that's as far as I know, certainly more than one. I wonder what happened to the others?'

'Dead. They are all dead.' It was the German who spoke. David and Tucky looked at him in amazement.

'You speak English?' said Tucky.

'I speak English,' said the German, leaning back in the chair and shutting his eyes. 'I speak very good English.' And he did; there was an accent, but it was barely discernible.

'But I thought . . .' Tucky remembered Mr

Reynolds. 'That's the first time, Mr Reynolds, honest. He never said a word in English before, not a word.'

Mr Reynolds got up from the table and crouched down by the German's chair. 'The other men in the plane,' he said, 'are they all dead?'

'All of them,' the German said, opening his eyes and looking at Mr Reynolds. 'All of them, dead. My plane sunk under the ground; there was no time, I could not get them out.'

'And the blankets,' Mr Reynolds held up the one that was drying by the stove. 'Where did you get these from?' David and Tucky held their breath. David felt his nails biting into the palms of his hands, and his heart pounded in his ears.

'I was cold and I was hungry,' he spoke clearly. 'I stole them. This afternoon and yesterday afternoon I came here. The house was empty, there was no one here. I took blankets, eggs, whisky, anything I could find. I am sorry to steal from your house, but when a man is that hungry he will do anything. I had to eat.'

Mr Reynolds straightened up and put his hands on his hips. 'You were bombing Plymouth last week?'

'I can say nothing about that.' The German leant back and closed his eyes again.

'Well, my dears,' Mr Reynolds was smiling. 'I'm beginning to understand it now. Jip must've followed him back out on to the moor, and I sent you two out after Jip. Well, I'll be blowed. You wouldn't believe it, would you? I'll tell you something, they'll never believe it in the village, my dears, not till they see him anyway.' He looked at the German and back at the boys. 'Well, I'll be blowed. I'll be blowed.'

The German had cleared them on every count, and the boys could relax for the first time. David was tempted to catch his eye, to thank him, but he dared not take the risk. There was no point in spoiling it now, not just for a gesture. He felt Tucky smiling at him confidentially, and he ignored him. They were safe, but he felt no triumph, only relief.

8

It was not long before Ann came back with three soldiers and an officer from Okehampton. It was the same officer who had led the search the week before, the one with the mean face and thin moustache. David and Tucky grinned at him, but the officer ignored them, and looked frostily at Mr Reynolds when he said that two boys and a dog had succeeded when the army, the police and the Home Guard had failed. The boys enjoyed his obvious embarrassment.

The German remained silent as they took him away, but as he was leaving the cottage he turned and saluted, and the boys noticed his eyes were smiling as he did so. Then he was gone and the soldiers with him. Tucky begged to be allowed to go up to the village with the soldiers, but was told that the prisoner was being taken directly to Okehampton for questioning. There was to be no glory that night for Tucky.

But it came the next day. At school assembly Mr Cooper congratulated David and Tucky on their courage and tenacity, and the entire school clapped and cheered them. In the middle of morning lessons, two men from the local paper arrived to interview them and to take photographs. Tucky did most of the talking now, and David only interrupted him when he thought Tucky might be forgetting which story he was telling. Overnight the 'townies' had become local heroes, and the village crowed over their two boys who had surprised and captured a burly German pilot by themselves.

At home Mr Reynolds killed one of the old hens for a celebration supper, and Ann baked a rhubarb pie. It was the crest of the wave. But through it all, David could not help thinking about the German pilot up on the moor fighting his way through the wind and rain towards the coast, and the happier the evening became, the more he thought of the lies and trickery that had made it all possible.

Neither of them could sleep that night. Tucky, too, was thinking about the German out on the moor. 'How far d'you think he's got?'

'Dunno,' said David. 'Not far; he can't have got far.'

108

'He won't die, will he?' Tucky said. 'I don't want him to die, do you?'

'No,' David said. 'I don't, course I don't, but I don't want him to get away either.'

'Do you think anyone knows, Davey; about him, I mean?'

'Not now, not after what that German told Mr Reynolds.'

'I suppose he was trying to thank us, d'you think?'

'S'pose so.'

'Davey, I like being liked, don't you? Everyone liked us today, at school, in the village, here – everyone.'

'D'you think Ann and Mr Reynolds would like us if they ever found out?' David asked quietly.

'Doesn't matter, does it?' Tucky said, knocking his pillow into shape. 'They'll never find out, not now, not ever.'

'I hope not.' David squeezed his eyes tight shut. 'I hope not.'

It was nearly a week later and they were having their tea with Ann when Mr Reynolds came back from market with the newspaper. He spread it out on the kitchen table and stood back.

'There you are, my dears,' he said. 'Famous at last. You put the village on the front page of the *Western Morning News* – 'tis the first time I've seen that.'

David and Tucky stared at their photograph. They were standing by the school gates. Tucky was grinning happily and giving the thumbs-up sign and he had his arm round David who was looking windswept and camera-shy.

The headline stood out in thick black lettering: 'Luftwaffe Pilot Captured by Village Boys.' And below was the story as Tucky had told it. They read it once and Tucky read it all through again, counting up the number of times his name was mentioned.

'They've cut it out and pinned it up on the wall in the village hall,' said Mr Reynolds. 'Like Ann and me, they're really proud of you.'

There was something in Mr Reynolds' voice that worried David. He glanced at Tucky to see if he had noticed it, but he hadn't. 'There's something else that might interest you,' he said from over his shoulders. 'Inside of the back page, let me turn it over.' He reached past them. 'There. There 'tis, where it says "German Airman Surrenders to Milkman". See it? You can read it if you'd like. 'Tis a good story, almost as good as yours.'

It was under the 'Late News' column down the side of the page, and it read: 'Milkman Harry Reddaway of Belstone on his rounds in

111

the village this morning was approached by a man claiming to be the pilot of a German bomber that crashed on the moor a fortnight ago. He said his plane had sunk in a bog and asked to be taken to the police. Mr Reddaway says the man was suffering from exposure. Police and army authorities believe he is from the same plane as the Luftwaffe pilot captured recently near Imberleigh, by two evacuee boys from London.'

David's mouth was dry when he'd finished reading it. He swallowed hard, and tried to speak normally. 'But he said they were all dead, didn't he? He said he was the only one left.'

''Tis natural enough, my dear. You'd hardly expect him to give his friend away, would you? 'Tis natural for a friend to protect a friend, isn't it? He was lying to us I'm afraid – about that anyway. No reason to lie about the rest, had he?'

There was no doubt now; at that moment both David and Tucky knew they were discovered. This time there was no quick answer, no way out. It was over. Only Ann looked puzzled. Mr Reynolds put his arm round her. ''Tis a little secret, Ann my dear, 'tis between Davey, Tucky and me, and that's an end of it. When they're ready no doubt they'll tell me why they did what they did, and then I can tell you, my dear.'

'He saved my life.' David felt his eyes warm with tears.

'We had to help them, just a little bit. He went in the river after Davey. We had to.' Tucky couldn't look them in the face.

Mr Reynolds nodded. 'I thought 'twould be something like that,' he said. 'They're fine boys, Ann. We often said that, haven't we, Ann? We often think that if we'd been blessed with children, we'd want to have them just like you two, and there's nothing'll change my mind.'

'You'll tell Ann?' David asked. 'You'll tell her everything?'

'Course I will, Davey, course I will, and then it'll be a secret between us all.'

'Was it wrong?' Tucky said quietly.

''Tis never wrong to do what you feel is right, Tucky,' said Mr Reynolds, ruffling his hair. 'Now, there's work to be done. There's a sheep or two gone out over the hedge on Back Meadow. Can you lend a hand, my dears?'

'Only one thing,' Mr Reynolds went on as they herded the sheep in through the gate, 'That bottle of whisky. I can forget the eggs, and Ann here, I expect she can forget her pie; but the whisky, that's a different matter. I won that in a raffle, that bottle, and I was going to make it last till the end of the war. You owe me one bottle of whisky – and when you're older and wiser and the war's all over, and past, perhaps you'd let me have it back, would you, my dears?'

And they did.

Today over thirty years later, Ann and Mr Reynolds have left the farm and moved up into a cottage in the village. Every year David and Tucky still come down to see them, and always when they come they bring Mr Reynolds his bottle of whisky. For Ann and Mr Reynolds it's the highlight of the year when their two 'children' from London, just the same but perhaps older and wiser, sit down in Ann's kitchen and remember the time when they helped Churchill win the war.

MICHAEL MORPURGO

War Horse

In the summer of 1914 Albert was growing up on his father's farm in Devon with a young horse he called Joey. In Germany Friedrich was at work in his butcher's shop. In France little Emilie played with her brothers in their orchard. But the clouds of war were on the horizon, and the armies gathered, drawing them all into a nightmare from which there was no escape.

'The **Black Beauty** of the Great War . . . Joey's marvellous horse's eye view of the 1914-18 holocaust may remain a favourite long after other runners and winners have been retired.'
   TIMES EDUCATIONAL SUPPLEMENT

MICHAEL MORPURGO

Mr Nobody's Eyes

For ten-year-old Harry, life has not been the same since his widowed mother remarried – especially now there is a new baby. In trouble at school, and feeling that no-one at home understands or has time for him, Harry runs away with his only friend in the world, a chimp from the circus. He and the mischievous Ocky share many exciting adventures, hitch a train ride and make friends with gypsies, facing dangers, betrayal and even death.

This is an exciting and warm story about loss and belonging, by a master storyteller. Michael Morpurgo is the author of a number of children's books including *King of the Cloud Forests* which was commended for the Carnegie Medal 1987 and *My Friend Walter*, shortlisted for the Smarties Prize in 1988.

MICHAEL MORPURGO

My Friend Walter

Bess Throckmorton is more than a little
surprised to learn that she is related to Sir
Walter Raleigh.

It is not long after this discovery that she
meets a mysterious man who takes her to the
Tower of London. She is sworn to secrecy and
must never reveal his identity. Bess loves her
new friend dearly until one day he vanishes,
just as her whole life is crumbling. Her father
is in disgrace and they have to sell their farm
lock, stock and barrel.

It isn't until they hear a news flash
announcing the robbery of one of the Crown
Jewels that their whole destiny changes.